Blair the Winner!
Theresa Breslin
Illustrated by
Ken Cox
D0307417
Mammoth

Also in the MAMMOTH STORYBOOK series:

Magic Betsey Malorie Blackman
The Tricky Tricky Twins Kate Elizabeth Ernest
Little Mouse Grandma Julia Jarman

First published in Great Britain in 1997
by Mammoth, an imprint of Egmont Children's Books Limited
239 Kensington High Street, London W8 6SA

'Blair . . . the boy who could not be still'
first published in 1995 in *Dear Mum, Don't Panic!*,
edited by Tony Bradman

ISBN 0 7497 2753 5

10 9 8

A CIP catalogue record for this book
is available from the British Library

Printed in Great Britain by Cox & Wyman Ltd,
Reading, Berkshire

Contents

~

For Dominic Andrew Michael Vaughan,
the boy who could not be still.

1 There was once a boy . . .

'Blair, give Willis one of your sweets,' said his mum as the three of them came out of the supermarket. She lifted Baby Willis from the shopping trolley and secured him in his buggy. 'You know those are his favourites.'

'They're all finished now,' said Blair, shoving the remainder of the packet of chocolate

minties deep into his pocket. He looked at his mum. 'I think,' he added quickly.

'Well, I *don't* think,' said Blair's mum. She put the shopping bags on the tray under the buggy. 'Blair,' she said, 'do you remember what I told you about sharing?'

'Yes,' mumbled Blair.

'And what did I tell you?' his mum asked as they began to walk along the street.

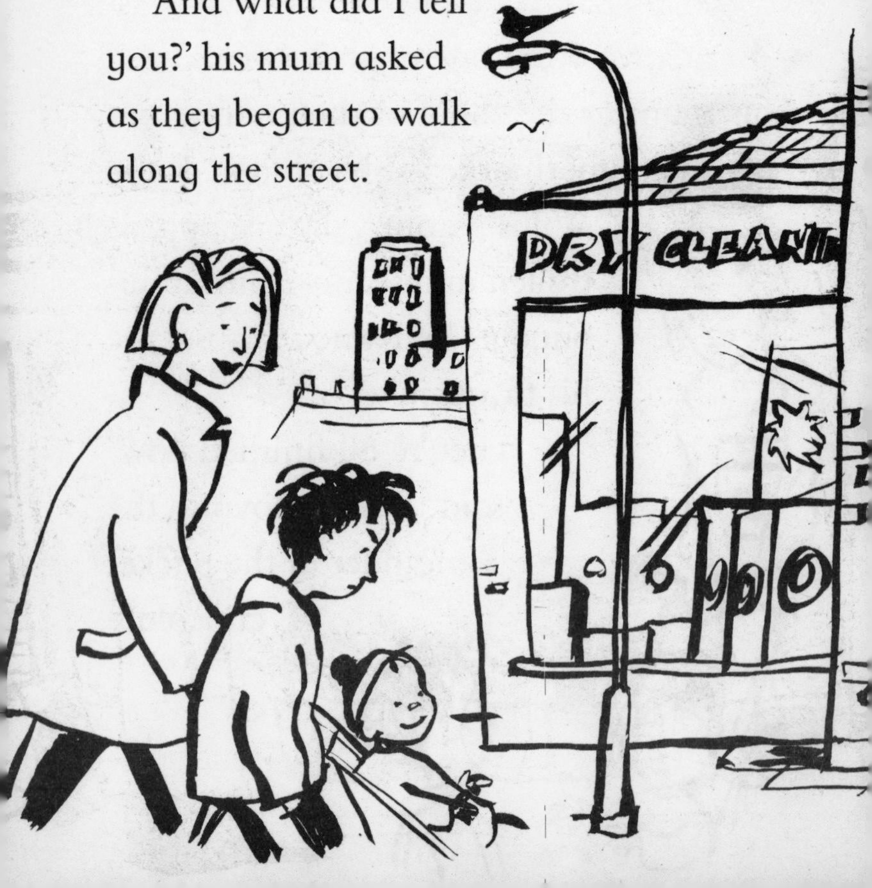

'That it's better when we share things with each other,' said Blair.

'That's a good boy.' His mum smiled at him. 'Now, do you want to share your sweets with your baby brother?'

'No,' said Blair, 'I don't.'

'You do really,' said his mum encouragingly.

'No, I don't,' said Blair truthfully.

'Yes you do,' said his mum. She stopped the buggy and prised Blair's fingers from round the packet of minties.

Then she took one and popped it into Willis's mouth.

'Glugg!' gurgled Willis.

Blair glared at his younger brother all the way home.

'We must discuss this as a family,' declared Blair's mum later that evening.

Blair's dad groaned. He had just pushed Melissa, Blair's big sister, from the couch on to the living-room floor and stretched himself out for a lie down.

'Must we?' he asked.

'Yes,' said Blair's mum firmly. 'We have to let Blair understand how important and worthwhile it is to share things.' She picked up her book and smiled at her husband.

'Explain it to him dear,' she said.

'Well, son,' said Blair's dad slowly, 'it's like this . . . Emm . . . Well, you know how I play football and I'm not a bad player, if I do say so myself.' He glanced quickly around the room. Melissa and Mum were reading, while Blair's granny had just begun knitting a woollie hat for Willis. Blair's dad lowered his voice. 'In fact, I'm quite talented in soccer skills, semi-professional . . . almost . . . Anyway, I take you to the park and we share a game together, and I let you have a go with my best leather football, signed by the World Cup squad.' Blair's dad nodded once or twice. 'So there you are, that's how it works. Sharing is better

than not sharing. OK, son?' He leaned over and ruffled Blair's hair. 'OK?'

'No,' said Blair, 'that's not true. I hardly ever get the ball. You always kick it up high where I can't reach it. *And* you want to score all the goals, and I never get to win a game.'

Blair's dad's face went quite pink. He quickly lay back on the couch and closed his eyes.

'Really, Andy!' Blair's mum tutted. I'm surprised at you!'

It is always the same, thought Blair. *He* was supposed to share but nobody was prepared to share with *him*.

He had once tried to taste one of Baby Willis's bicky rusks.

But when he reached his hand into the pram, Willis had BITTEN him, really hard, on his index finger. Dad had said that, in future, if Blair wanted a bicky rusk it would be a lot more sensible to choose one that Willis wasn't actually eating at the time. Mum had said Willis was only trying out his very first tooth, and that Blair's finger looked exactly like a bicky rusk to Willis.

But Blair knew the truth.

Willis had decided *he* wasn't sharing. Blair examined his finger carefully. If you looked closely enough you could still see the mark.

Even Blair's granny, who was normally very kind indeed, had objected quite strongly when Blair had borrowed her false teeth. He had meant to keep them for a few seconds only, so that they could be the Mega-Big-Brontosaurus gobbling up his defenceless little Legoland people. How was he to know that gran didn't have a spare set of teeth, and that she had just laid them down for a minute in the bathroom before rushing out to Cousin Gertrude's wedding? Then, what with everybody shouting at him, he couldn't recall where he had left them until two days later.

Granny had forgiven him, and brought him a piece of wedding cake from the reception. She said she couldn't manage to eat the icing anyway just at present.

'Melissa sometimes shares things with you,' said his mum.

Blair thought about this.

He remembered at Easter when he had wanted a piece of Melissa's super-duper milk chocolate egg, which a very special boyfriend had given her. It was so huge he thought she'd never miss the tiny piece he had nibbled, but she had *screeched* and *screeched* about it for ages.

Blair was sure she must have examined it all over with a magnifying glass for her to spot his teeth marks.

Then there was the time she had gone *berserk* when he had taken her talcum powder to make a very small blizzard for his Fighting Fantasy Figures to wade through on their journey to the land of Lir ... And, on another occasion, he had needed blood marks on his magic sword to prove that he had slain the Deadly Dragon of Doom. It wasn't his fault that the lid of her ruby-red nail varnish didn't screw back on properly, and that it had spilled out all over her new duvet cover.

Just recently she had made the most dreadful fuss when he had borrowed her black shawl to be Dracula at a fancy dress party. Granny had told him privately that you would hardly notice the hole he had cut in the middle for his head to fit through.

And only yesterday – he stopped. Perhaps they hadn't found out about yesterday yet . . .

'No she doesn't,' said Blair. 'Melissa doesn't share with me.'

'Too right,' said Melissa. She leaped to her feet and tossed her hair back from her face. 'And what is more, I have no intention of *ever* sharing *anything* with that monster. If you think for one minute that I'm going to allow a grotty little boy with grubby fingers anywhere near any of my possessions, then you are *wrong*, *wrong*, *wrong*.'

'Are you quite sure now, Melissa?' asked her dad.

He opened one eye and looked up at her.

'I mean, you wouldn't want to say "wrong" one more time in order to clear up any doubts we might have? Was that your final word on the subject?'

'No! It is not my final word!' declared Melissa. She pointed at Blair. 'I will thank you to tell that child to stay away from my things.' She flounced out of the living-room slamming the door behind her.

They heard the sound of Melissa's feet stamping upstairs.

'She doesn't really mean that,' Blair's mum said soothingly.

'I was convinced,' muttered Blair's dad from the couch.

'Sharing is not good,' said Blair.

'There is *nothing* that is better when shared.' He folded his arms across his chest.

'*Absolutely nothing.*'

'I might know something,' said his granny quietly from her corner by the fire. She put her knitting down. She had a faraway look in her eyes.

'Something that people, all over the world, love to share and they do it all the time.'

'What?' demanded Blair,

'Come here and I'll share it with you, and then you can tell me if you agree.' She moved over and made a space in her big armchair.

'What is it?' asked Blair as he climbed up beside her.

'I wonder if you can guess,' said his granny. 'Are you listening?'

'Yes,' said Blair.

Blair's granny opened her mouth and started to speak. 'Once upon a time . . . ' she began.

'A story!' cried Blair.

'Clever boy!' said his granny. She looked at him. 'Would you like me to share it with you?'

'Yes,' said Blair.

'And then will you share one with me?' she asked him.

Blair nodded. He gave his gran a hug. Perhaps, just perhaps, some things were good to share. 'Tell me your story, Granny,' he said.

'Well,' she said slowly. 'Let me see now . . . Once upon a time there was a boy called . . .' She stopped speaking. 'Mmmm . . . let me think. Oh, yes, I know!' She put her arm round Blair and drew him close in beside her. 'There was once a boy,' she said, 'a very smart boy, brave and sensible. And his name was . . .' She paused and looked down. '. . . his name was Blair!' she said. 'Now, I'm going to tell you some stories about him . . .'

2

Blair . . . the boy who could not be still

The problem with Blair Matthews was that he could never be still.

Every day, as soon as the first rays of the sun touched his face, Blair would give a great whoop and leap out of bed . . . knocking over the bedside lamp, a jigsaw puzzle, his favourite storybook, and spilling last night's mug of cocoa all over the carpet.

'Oh no!' moaned the rest of the family, and they shut their eyes tightly and burrowed right down under their blankets.

You could tell Blair's house from all the others in the street. It was the one with the burnt-out potting shed, the cracked windows, and the garden fence broken in several places.

During the summer Blair always helped out with the family barbecues. The village fire-fighters had told Blair's mum that the fire-engine could

probably find the way to Blair's house by itself now.

Blair also liked to play cricket, although he knew he wasn't the best batsman in the world, or even the second best. His granny said for him not to worry. If he kept practising he was bound to improve. So he did.

Then there was the garden fence, which was broken in several places. Blair had offered to fix it, now he had given up training to be an Olympic hurdler, but his mum and dad said it was all right. They said they were fed up mending it anyway, and they were going to grow a hedge instead. A very prickly hawthorn hedge.

Mr and Mrs Higgins, who owned the local D-I-Y repair shop, always sent Blair's family an extra-large card at Christmas-time.

One Sunday morning, Blair charged down the stairs for breakfast.

He tripped over the dog and stood on the cat's tail.

He raced into the kitchen and clambered up on to his chair.

The budgie moved quickly to the furthest corner of his cage.

His mother put a soft-boiled egg in front of him. Blair grabbed his bread soldiers for dunking.

'Blair,' said his mum, 'be carefu –'

'Watch out, Blair!' cried his dad.

'How did that happen?' asked Blair, looking at the blobs of yellow egg yolk spattered on his clean white T-shirt. He scrambled quickly down from his chair to get a cloth from the sink, pulling the tablecover and all the dishes with him.

'That boy is a walking disaster area,' said his dad, mopping up the mess.

'A pain in the neck,' said his big sister picking her slice of toast out of the dog's dish.

'EEEEK!' said Baby Willis, and he crawled away under the table as fast as he could.

'He's an active wee chappie, isn't he?' his granny said fondly, as Blair rushed outside to play. 'Would you look at him now?' she added proudly.

Blair was galloping round and round the garden being an Arab horseman.

'He must have ants in his pants,' his mum said wearily.

‘He should grow out of this stage soon,’ said his dad.

‘He may never get the opportunity,’ said his big sister, Melissa, running outside and snatching her best white cotton nightie from Blair’s head.

At teatime Blair came indoors. His face was pink and he was out of breath.

‘I think I’ll go and lie down,’ he said.

‘Whatever for?’ asked Melissa in amazement.

‘Perhaps now we’ll get some peace and quiet,’ said Blair’s dad.

‘It’s when they’re quiet, that’s the time to worry,’ said his granny.

‘Nonsense,’ said Blair’s mum.

‘He’s probably just a little tired.’

The next morning there was a deep silence from Blair’s room. The rest of the house woke up slowly.

'Do you hear anything?' asked Blair's mum.

'Nothing at all,' said his dad.

They looked at each other in alarm. Then they got up quickly and went into Blair's bedroom. Blair lay in bed. His face was red and blotchy.

'I don't want to get up today,' he said.

'I'd better call the doctor,' said his mum in a very strained voice.

'I don't think he's very well.

'Told you so,' said his granny smugly.

The doctor came. 'Measles,' she said. 'Plenty of rest.'

So Blair stayed in bed for four days. He said he felt awful.

So did the rest of the family.

'You fairly miss the wee one running about,' said his granny, and dropped three stitches of her knitting.

'The house is terribly quiet,' said Blair's mum.

'Life can get boring,' said Blair's dad, staring out of the window.

'Everything in my room is exactly where I left it,' said Melissa tetchily. 'I can't find anything.'

Willis whimpered quietly and sucked the end of his sleeve.

On Friday, Blair said, 'I feel lots better.'

On Saturday, he sat up in bed.

Next morning, very early, there was a loud crash from downstairs, and a strong smell of burning toast. The family hurried down to the kitchen and cautiously opened the door. A box of breakfast cereal lay on its side with the contents spilled out all over the worktop.

The fridge door was open and a large lake of milk was spreading slowly across the floor.

'Ooops,' said Blair. 'Sorry.'

And he waited to be told off . . .

Everbody smiled at Blair.

'That's all right, son,' said Blair's dad, and he patted him on the head. Then he looked down at his hand, and, picking up a tea-towel, he carefully wiped his jam-smeared fingers one by one.

Blair's mum stepped back from the puddle of milk, which was lapping round her slippers. 'You're feeling better then, pet?' she said, and her worried voice had gone away completely.

'Thank goodness this house is normal again,' said Blair's sister. 'Now I can get some sleep.'

'Glug. Glug,' agreed Baby Willis.

The family went back upstairs to bed where they put their fingers in their ears, shut their eyes tightly and burrowed right down under the blankets.

3 Blair goes camping

'This is the life,' said Blair's dad.

He stood at the door of their brand new family tent and breathed in deeply. Then he gazed across to where the river flowed quietly beside a shingly beach. All around him the forest trees grew tall and straight, and the sun beat down.

'Perfect spot for camping,' he said. 'Perfect.'

'Except that no one wants to go camping, apart from you,' grumbled Blair's granny. She pushed past Blair's dad and walked towards the water with her portable TV set in one hand and her deckchair in the other. 'I'm going to miss the big snooker game tonight,' she said. 'It's not the same when you watch it in black and white.' She took several minutes to get her deckchair to sit steadily on the pebbles, then she sat herself down, and switched on her television.

'The outdoor life is much more healthy,' declared Blair's dad. 'Being cooped up inside during the weeks and weeks of sunshine wasn't good for us. It was time to get away for the weekend.'

'Yes, but you didn't need to rush off and buy a tent,' said Blair's mum.

'We could have stayed in a small hotel or guest-house, and gone for long walks.'

'It's not the same,' said Blair's dad. He inhaled deeply. 'Smell that wonderful fresh air.'

'Aaaaachoooo!'
said Blair's mum.
'Aachoo!
Aachoo!
Aachoo!'

She plonked
Baby Willis
down, pulled out a
hankie and dabbed at
her watering eyes.
'My hay fever's started now,'
she said.

Baby Willis grabbed some earth with his fingers and scooped it up into his mouth.

'Right, Blair,'
said Dad.

‘We’re going to make a campfire. You gather twigs for kindling and I’ll collect some branches. We’ll cook the grub over the fire, then we’ll sit and sing songs round the embers as evening falls.’

There was a loud snort from the direction of granny’s deckchair.

Blair began to search around for some suitable kindling for their fire. Just then his big sister, Melissa, pulled aside the tent flap and came outside. She had her curling brush dangling by the cord from her hand.

‘Where do I plug this in?’ she asked.

‘There isn’t any electricity,’ said her dad. ‘We are camping properly, as close to nature as we can get.’

Melissa shrugged. ‘I suppose I can use my gas-filled one but I need a new canister. Where are the shops?’ she said.

‘The nearest shop,’ said Blair’s mum carefully, ‘is sixty miles away.’

‘Sixty miles!’ said Melissa. ‘Sixty miles! You are joking! I always go round the shops on a Saturday. What am I going to do tomorrow?’

‘We’ll go on a trek,’ said Blair’s dad firmly. ‘Much more fun.’

Melissa rolled her eyes. ‘We’ll see about that,’ she said. She swatted a midgie on her arm and peered around her. ‘Where’s the loo then?’ she asked.

Blair’s mum looked at his dad. ‘Melissa is asking where the toilets are dear,’ she said. ‘Explain it to her, will you?’ Then

Blair's mum picked up Baby Willis, cleaned out his mouth and went to join Gran by the water's edge.

Blair's dad lowered his voice to speak to Melissa. Blair saw him point to an old shovel lying beside the tent, then his dad pointed to the bushes. He pointed to the bushes several times.

'NO WAY!' shrieked Melissa.

A flock of birds shot up out of the nearest tree and took off to the north, cawing madly.

'No way!' said Melissa. '*No way, no way, no way.*' Then she stomped back into the tent and refused to come out again.

Blair found a really good place to collect firewood.

Just behind where dad had parked his car someone had thoughtfully gathered lots of long twigs and thin dry branches. There was a kind of framed trestle with a sign on it where these bundles of kindling with long poles in the middle had been carefully laid out. Blair pulled the poles out and put them aside. He thought that they would make good swords for later. Then he broke off a few large chunks of the twigs and sped off towards his dad.

'Excellent, excellent,' said his dad, tottering back from the other direction with an armful of larger pieces of wood.

'I don't know about this, dear,' said Blair's mum. 'Perhaps we should have brought a Primus stove. It will take ages to cook the food over an open fire.'

'Nonsense,' said Blair's dad confidently. 'I know what I am doing.'

As soon as the fire was lit Blair's dad put a pan of food and some sausages on skewers on top of the flames. A long plume of smoke drifted above the tops of the trees.

'More sticks needed, son,' said his dad. He tried to turn one of the sausages. It fell off on to the fire.

Blair rushed back to the place where he had found the bundles gathered up so neatly. As he grabbed another chunk he suddenly noticed the sign . . .

He raced back to the campfire.

'Dad,' he said. 'Dad, dad, dad –'

'Hush, son,' said Blair's dad crossly. Another sausage had slid from its skewer and was now burning merrily. 'I'm concentrating at the moment.'

'Dad, I need to tell you . . .' began Blair.

'Please be quiet,' said Blair's dad. He tried to snatch at the third and fourth sausages as they fell on to the fire.'

'I think –' said Blair.

'Well don't,' snapped his dad. He stuck his burnt fingers in his mouth.

'Dad,' said Blair.

'Enough!' His dad glared at him. The bottom of the frying-pan was turning black. Blair's dad picked it up by the handle, then dropped it with a yelp. Most of its contents emptied out on to the grass. 'I forbid you to say another word!'

'But . . .' said Blair.

'NOT ONE SINGLE WORD!' Blair's dad shouted.

Blair opened his mouth and then closed it again. He waggled his arms about. He jumped up and down. He even stood on his head.

'Look at the child,' said Blair's mum.

Blair's granny looked. 'Do you think he's trying to tell us something?' she said.

By this time Blair was running round in circles.

DAD!!

'I don't think so,' said Blair's mum. 'He always carries on like that.'

Blair's face was purple. He made windmill actions with his arms and blew his cheeks out with great puffing noises.

The whole family stared at him. Baby Willis's mouth dropped open and a long dribble slid down his chin.

Granny put her head to one side. 'Well if you're sure,' she said slowly. She turned back to her television programme.

Blair raced to the car and took something out of the boot. He ran back to the campfire and, pulling the lever of the portable fire extinguisher, he skooshed it all over the flames.

'What do you think you're doing?' roared his father in a loud angry voice.

'What do you think *you* are doing?' roared an even louder and angrier voice.

The forest ranger came charging into the clearing. 'We've had a six-week drought and there are signs everywhere forbidding fires. Are you trying to burn down the whole forest?' he yelled at Blair's dad.

'I think that ranger was most unreasonable,' complained Blair's dad on the drive home that night. 'There was

absolutely no need for him to shout as loudly as that, and for so long.'

'It may have been the fact that you used the special brooms they make for beating fires out as kindling for your own fire that annoyed him so much,' said Blair's mum.

'Blair has to take some blame for that,' said Blair's dad.

'No, it certainly was NOT Blair's fault,' said Blair's mum. 'As soon as he saw the "No Campfires" sign he tried to tell you, but you wouldn't listen.' She blew her nose. She hadn't sneezed for at

least ten minutes and her eyes had stopped streaming. She pulled Blair over beside her on the back seat of the car and gave him a special big cuddle and stroked his hair. 'Blair was extremely brave and quick-witted,' she said.

'He was a hero,' his gran told Mr and Mrs Higgins when they stopped off at the local D-I-Y shop to buy a refill for their fire extinguisher.

'Blair saved the day.' She looked at her watch. 'Better rush,' she said, 'snooker starts in ten minutes.' Then she bought Blair a pterodactyl from Mr Higgins's model tray.

Later that night Melissa came into Blair's room.

'Blair,' she said, 'camping skills like yours deserve a reward.' And she thrust something into Blair's hand.

Blair looked at the fifty pence piece. I like camping, he thought as he settled down to sleep. I'm going to ask Dad if we can go again tomorrow.

4

Blair's birthday party

On the morning of his birthday, Blair woke up at about four forty-five a.m. As soon as he opened his eyes he jumped out of bed and zoomed downstairs just to check if the postman had been.

He hadn't.

Blair went slowly back up the stairs. He flopped down on his bed, gave a huge sigh, and waited for ages and ages. Around five o' clock he jumped back out of bed and went down to the front door to have another look.

He gave an *enormous* sigh. Still no sign. He went back upstairs.

Blair tried again at five past five, ten past five, five-fifteen, five-sixteen, and five-twenty. And then again at five twenty one, two, three and four.

'Blair!' roared his dad. 'Go back to bed at once!'

Baby Willis began to cry. The dog whined to be let out. The cover slid off the budgie's cage and it began to chirrup.

'Oh no,' groaned the family.

'It's my birthday,' Blair told the boy who came with the morning milk.

'Cheers, mate,' said the milk boy.

'Today's my birthday,' he said to the girl who did the newspaper round.

'Happy birthday, Blair,' she said.

'This is a special day for me,' Blair informed the postman when he eventually appeared.

'I guessed as much,' said the postman and he handed Blair lots and lots of birthday cards. 'All the best, son.'

'I'm having a birthday party,' Blair told the WRVS lady who brought his granny's library books.

'Many happy returns of the day, young man,' she said and shook his hand.

By this time Blair had his face washed, hair brushed, and was wearing his new striped lime-green shirt, and a purple spotted bow tie.

'He looks very handsome,' the WRVS lady told his granny.

'Aye,' said Blair's granny proudly. 'He's a bonny boy.'

'What does bonny mean?' Blair asked Melissa.

'Good looking,' said his big sister, Melissa, 'attractive – like a film star.' She studied him for a moment or two. 'Er . . . Blair, when gran bought you the lime-green shirt, did she know that you meant to wear it with that particular tie?'

'Yes,' said Blair. 'We picked it specially to match, It's mega-bright, isn't it?' he said happily.

'I won't argue with that,' said Melissa.

'Granny is going to wear her orange straw hat to my party,' said Blair. 'The one with the plastic fruit and flowers round the brim.'

'I think *I'll* wear my sunglasses,' said Melissa.

* * *

Blair's guests arrived at three o' clock.

Samantha was first through the door.

'Give Blair his present,' said Samantha's mum.

'Don't want to,' said Samantha.

'Let's play some games,' said Blair's dad quickly.

They began with pinning the tail on the donkey. When his mum took his blindfold off, Blair saw his tail was stuck on the donkey's nose. Everybody giggled.

Then they played pass the parcel. Blair got stuck with the parcel immediately, and he was put out of the circle right away. He had to wait the longest of anyone until the game was finished.

When it was musical cushions and the music stopped, everyone raced to a cushion and sat down. Everyone except Blair. He didn't manage to grab one in time and he had to sit out first again.

Then they played Who am I? Gordon was first to go. He read from his card. 'I've got four hooves, antlers, and . . .'

'Your Bambi's daddy,' Blair called quickly.

'. . . and a red nose,' finished Gordon.

Everybody laughed at Blair.

'I'm Rudolph, silly,' said Gordon. 'And anyway you're not supposed to shout out.'

'Right,' said Blair's dad. 'We'll have some games in the garden now, while the food is set out on the big table.'

Blair pulled at his dad's sleeve. 'Dad,' he said. 'Can we play a game now that I will win?'

'They haven't invented that game yet, son,' said his dad.

Blair wandered into the kitchen and kicked the washing-machine.

'Are you enjoying the party?' his granny asked him.

'No,' said Blair. 'The games are rotten.'

'Dearie me,' said his granny. 'Dearie, dearie me.' She looked out of the window into the garden. 'What games

are they playing now?' she asked.

'Jumping with a balloon between your legs,' said Blair. 'Whoever can keep going the longest, without bursting their balloon, is the winner.'

Blair's gran stared out of the window for a minute or two. 'Hmm,' she said. She patted the plastic fruit on her straw hat. 'Hmm,' she said again. 'I think you should have a go at that game Blair.'

Blair shook his head.

Granny put her hand under his chin and fixed his bow tie. 'Go on,' she said, 'just for me. I've got a lucky feeling about this one.'

'I'll pass round some cakes while the children are jumping,' said Blair's granny.

'Is that a good idea?' asked Blair's mum.

Blair's granny nodded. 'Yes,' she said. 'It's a *very* good idea actually.'

She straightened her orange straw hat and went out into the garden.

BANG! went Gordon's balloon.

'Never mind, dear,' said Blair's granny who was standing beside him. 'Have a cake.'

BANG! went Samantha's balloon.

'Must have been a thorn from the rose bush,' said Blair's granny who happened to be passing with a plate in her hand. 'Choose a cake, pet.'

BANG! went Letty's balloon.

'Shame,' said Blair's granny from just behind her. 'A nice cake will cheer you up.'

BANG! BANG! BANG! went all the balloons in the garden. All except Blair's that is. Eventually he was the only person still jumping up and down with an unburst balloon.

'Blair's the winner!' declared his dad.

Blair's mum gave granny a long look. 'I noticed that you never offered Blair a cake,' she said. 'In fact, you didn't ever go near him at all during the game.'

'Indeed,' smiled Blair's granny.

Later, when no one was looking, Blair's granny stuck her hatpin back into her hat.

'I'm beginning to enjoy this party,' she said.

'So am I,' said Blair.